Lustman to the Rescue

Helen Walton

Walton House Publishing

www.helenwaltonauthor.com

Contents

A Short Story

♥

ONE MORE MINUTE IN this leather costume and I'd most likely strangle someone.

My friend Natalie, to be exact.

This dress-up Halloween party of hers was as uncomfortable as the other dress-up parties she threw on any occasion she could, but I'd fake excitement for my best friend. I'd faked a lot in my life, which came in handy being an actress, probably why I'd taken to acting classes like a natural. Kisses landed on my cheeks from inebriated friends as I walked rather awkwardly in the leather costume toward where I'd last seen Nat.

I searched the crowded room for Natalie since she'd vanished from the last place I'd seen her beside the punch bowl. It was time for me to say my goodbyes. I was out of here. I'd made it to the obligatory midnight like Cinderella about to turn back into a peasant. This freaking costume clung to me in places that were uncomfortable and stimulating at the same time. I might even strangle Natalie when I found her. She'd picked out the costumes. Batman and Robin for me and Jake, my other roommate. While Natalie dressed as Wonder Woman and her boyfriend, the famous Conrad Saint James, dressed as Superman. She was on a superhero kick right now after having landed a role in a movie. I was proud of her for breaking out from commercials. Meanwhile, Jake and I had recently auditioned for an upcoming sitcom and we were on tenterhooks waiting for the casting news.

My two housemates were my best friends along with my childhood best friend and neighbor Claire. Although we didn't see as much of Natalie as we used to now she spent a lot of time with Conrad. The party was a way of making sure we spent Halloween together. I didn't have a choice in accompanying them tonight in a costume. The things we do for the people we love. Like dressing up as Batman. Natalie had given me the choice of Cat Woman, but one glance at the skimpy costume online and I'd chosen the two-piece Batman suit.

What a poor decision that was. Black leather clung to my skin in a heated, sticky mess. As usual, I'd downed a few drinks to make being in costume in real life more bearable. I dressed up for a living and I didn't want to do it outside of work, but my first trip to the bathroom was catastrophic. I hadn't touched another sip since for fear I'd get stuck, half undressed, in the bathroom for the rest of the night.

I was so done with the night. If I ever saw a Batman costume again, I'd cringe and offer my sympathies to the wearer.

I pushed through the crowd, uncaring that my elbows dug in a little too much. No one noticed since they were too drunk to care. The stale, booze-soaked, perfume-filled, and sweaty air caught in the back of my throat. I spotted Natalie standing in a dark corner with her Superman boyfriend, looking like he was about to devour her. Good for her. At least someone would end the night with a bang.

"Nat," I yelled over the music and loud voices.

She smiled at me like all her Christmases had come at once. The love she'd developed for Conrad after nearly accidentally killing him made my heart glow with happiness. I'd high-five her, but it might look weird.

"I'm going."

"Don't go, Emily."

Nope, I wouldn't take her fun away from her. She'd spend the rest of her night with the love of her life. I wanted to go home and peel this leather costume off me. Unlike her, I'd attempt that task alone because I'd guarantee it wouldn't be sexy like her skimpy Wonder Woman costume.

I leaned into her ear. "Have fun."

"Oh, I will."

I left her party, fighting my way across the room and closer to the door. Escape was within reach. Next year I'd sit at home and feed trick-or-treaters candy while eating most of it myself. Who was I kidding? Nat wouldn't let me do that. What if I faked being sick? I'd have an entire year to plan my fake illness. I was an actress, I'd come up with something. An evil laugh bubbled up my throat and escaped as I stepped out into the street.

Oh, thank goodness, fresh air.

"What's so funny?"

I spun, startled by the deep voice behind me. I shouldn't have been. Jake the Rake was Robin to my Batman. His closely shaved black hair matched the black leather Robin eye mask. Deep blue eyes peered back at me framed by dark lashes that made many women gaze into them with longing. The mask drew attention to his lips and strong jaw, lips made for sinful pleasures. Everything about him was.

I hadn't seen him since we'd entered the party. I figured he'd scored early in his skin-tight Robin tights that left nothing to the imagination. Jake was hung, really and truly hung like a God. I may have caught a glimpse, or two, or three, while we'd been roomies. Couldn't blame a girl for looking. Seriously, it was hard to miss.

"Just planning an illness for next year's Halloween party."

"Count me in."

"What! No way. Nat won't let both of us miss Halloween."

"Damn straight. I'm done with these ridiculous costumes." He pulled at the crotch of his tights.

Did he have to bring my attention to his junk? Like the chaffing of the leather hadn't rubbed me enough tonight. And, okay, I had a serious crush on Jake, but he was a rake. I'd never seen him with the same woman twice.

And we were roomies. Don't shit where you eat, as the saying went.

"It can be contagious," he said.

I snorted and dragged my attention away from his impressive dick. Not for me. Maybe I'd text my ex, Daryl, and see if he'd be up for a booty call tonight, but what would be the point? He'd never made me come in the six months we'd been together. No man had.

"Contagious like syphilis?"

"You know that means we'd have to have sex?"

"I... well... ah, shut up."

Heat climbed a telling tale across my cheeks. As if I wasn't thinking about sex with him enough, he'd planted an even bigger image in my sex-starved mind. I bet he'd know how to make a woman come.

He chuckled. The sound raced down my spine like he'd trailed fingers over my skin. Holy hell, I needed to get out of this costume and away from Jake.

"I'm going home. I'll see you later."

Turning from Jake, I yanked my phone out of my pocket and summoned an Uber. Yes, Batman had pockets. It would only be minutes before a car arrived. Thank goodness for modern technology. Then I'd go home and try to take this damn infuriating leather costume off.

Jake rubbed the back of his neck as silence descended between us.

Awkward.

Why did he have to mention us having sex?

Relief shot through my veins when a car pulled up. I yanked the door open without a backward glance at Jake. Time to put the night behind me, so to speak. I reached for the door, but Jake was beside me and my hand hit him firmly in the stomach.

"What are you doing?"

"May as well catch a ride home with you."

His body heat filled my palm, and I snatched my hand back before I did something crazy like run it over his firm muscles. I scooted over to the other side of the car as far away from him as possible. He shot an odd look my way, but I turned from him and stared out the window.

"Are you drunk?"

"What? No." I shook my head.

"Why not? It's a party?"

"If you must know, I had trouble going to the bathroom in this damn leather costume."

He laughed. I turned and, thanks to his skin-tight costume, watched the deep ripples of his stomach muscles as they spasmed with his laughter.

"That I'd like to see."

"Hardy ha-ha." I scowled at him. "It's worse than trying to pull off wet swimsuit and trying to pull them back on. I thought I'd give myself a hernia with the struggle."

"Bloody Nat." He mocked a scowl.

"I'm thinking of retribution."

"Toothbrush in the toilet?"

"Nah, too tame."

"Hair remover in the conditioner?"

"Nah, too much. Maybe a laxative-laced brownie."

"You two are hilarious. I'm glad we're roomies."

"Me too," I admitted. I couldn't imagine never meeting Jake. He was fun and enjoyed our pranks and enjoyed being a part of them, too. The first time we'd pranked him, we hadn't been sure how he'd take the salt in the sugar bowl. Nat and I had hooted with laughter when he'd spat his coffee over the kitchen table. When he realized what we'd done, he laughed with us. Later that day, he'd attacked us with water pistols, and we'd known he'd fit right in.

The Uber pulled to a stop at our humble abode, a small three-bedroom house in a quiet suburban neighborhood not too far from the city. When my parents decided to sell up and go traveling I'd jumped at the chance to live close to the college but soon realized I needed more income to pay for the bills and the mortgage. Hence my two roommates.

Jake scooted out of the car and I slid along the seat, biting back a moan as the movement made the leather costume rub against my sensitive parts. Damn costume.

Even walking to the front door rubbed and I couldn't stop myself from admiring the firm roundness of Jake's butt in the tights. I'd love to take a bite out of them or dig my fingernails into them.

I was officially crazy with lust for the man, and he had no clue.

Jake opened the door and flicked on the entry light, then turned to me.

"Do you want a drink?"

"Nah, all I want to do is get out of this leather."

He rubbed the back of his neck again and lifted the leather mask from his face.

"Em?"

"Yeah?"

He shook his head. "Goodnight."

An odd tingle radiated out of my stomach. What was he going to ask?

"Goodnight, Robin," I said cheekily and turned to the hallway leading to the bedrooms.

Thank goodness my bedroom was connected to the three-way bathroom. I ducked in there first to relieve myself and with pants around my thighs, I shuffled out to the sink and prayed Jake was in the kitchen or his bedroom and wouldn't get a clear view of my blindingly white ass, because there was no way I'd pull these leather pants back up even if I wanted to, which I didn't. I never wanted to see leather again.

The scent was pleasant, though. That was all I could say about wearing leather.

I shuffled into my bedroom and sat on the side of my bed. Now to get the pants off all the way. The struggle was real. I tugged on the material, and they rolled over themselves, making an even bigger and more complicated mess of removing them. Giving up trying to pull them off from my thighs, I turned to the ankles after I removed my boots. I fell back on the bed with my struggles. How hard could this be? I wriggled around like a freaking butterfly trying to emerge out of a cocoon. So not pretty.

I lay back, panting and regaining my strength for another attempt. Had I even moved them a fraction? They were stuck on my calves. I swung a leg up in the air and with an almighty yank the leather moved, and I tumbled off the bed, letting out a startled scream. The top half of me landed with a loud thud on the timber floorboards.

"Ouch," I whimpered.

LUSTMAN TO THE RESCUE

A loud knock sounded on my bedroom door. I tried to move, but it was impossible with one arm stuck behind my back and my legs propped up on the side of the bed. I was half hanging from the bed.

"Emily, are you okay in there?"

"I'm fine," I yelled.

A cold sweat formed on my brow. Bad enough I was stuck in my leather costume. Now I was stuck and hanging from the side of my bed. The last thing I needed right now was Jake to come in and see me like this. I needed Natalie. No, I needed Claire. She'd been my best friend since primary school. She wouldn't bat an eyelash at helping me when I was half-naked, but Jake, nope, no freaking way.

I placed my free hand on the timber floorboards and pushed, trying to free my other arm. It didn't work. My arm remained stuck under my back, leather glued to leather, much like my pants.

"Shit!"

"Em, you don't sound okay. I'm coming in."

"No!"

The door creaked open, and I placed my free hand over my eyes, trying to hide my mortification. If I didn't see him, I'd pretend Jake didn't see me.

"Jake, get out. I'm half-naked."

"I see that," he said, "but you look impressively stuck."

"I'll figure it out in a minute. Just leave."

"Not before I get a photo first."

"What the hell?" I moved my hand to curse him more, but he didn't have his phone in his hand.

"Come on, you've got to admit it's funny." He grinned.

"Hardy ha-ha. See how much I'm laughing, you jerk."

"Jerk? Wow, is that what I get for coming in here to help? I'll just leave you to it, then."

He backed up to the door but didn't turn around. His gaze focused on my half-clad legs.

"Wait, I'm sorry, can you please help?" I asked. What was the point of denying his help now? He'd seen me in this mortifying situation. I may as well go the whole way.

"Sure thing."

He bounded across the room like an excited puppy and jumped on the bed.

"Ah, what are you doing?"

"I'm helping."

He slid his hand to my left ankle. Warmth skated along my skin at his touch, and he eased the leather free easily. As my left leg was freed from the confining leather, it fell from the side of the bed and joined me at an odd angle on the floor.

Jake's eyes followed the movement as his fingers gripped my right ankle. Oh, dear Lord, I was now spread-legged in front of him. Heat burned every inch of my skin. Could tonight get any worse?

I squeezed my eyes shut. Yep, time to pretend none of this was happening.

"Em," he said, throatily, "you have the prettiest pussy I've ever seen."

What?

I snapped my eyelids open. Jake was staring straight at my hoo-ha. The scorching, embarrassing heat turned to a different heat under his intense gaze. My bits, which the leather had rubbed all night, throbbed in need and roared to life with a burning hunger for Jake. My inner muscles clenched in a need to have him fill me.

"Did you just wink at me?"

"What? No." I was sure I hadn't winked.

His tongue darted out to his lips and my thoughts turned to his tongue on me. My inner muscles clenched again.

"There. You did it again." His hand tightened on my ankle.

"I did not," I huffed, knowing I hadn't winked that time.

"I'm sure you did." He slid a hand up my leg and traced a finger along the edge of the leather on my calf. "Do you want me?"

"What? No." I gulped. His fingers scorched a trail of need straight to my core.

"I want to lick your pretty pussy and find out if it tastes as good as it looks."

Holy hell, that was hot. My inner muscles clenched, and moisture flooded me. I'd never in my life been so turned on by a man and we hadn't even kissed or touched intimately.

"There it is again. Your pussy keeps winking at me."

I sucked in oxygen like I was starved of it. He tugged the leather pants from my right leg, not letting go with his hand, then leaned over the side of the bed and my heart skipped a beat, thinking he was about to follow through on his words. His warm breath skated over my intimate flesh and another clench of desire rocked me.

"Damn, Em, I've wanted you for a long time."

"You have?" I squeaked. How was a logical thought possible with his face so close to my aching hoo-ha?

"Yep, why do you think I don't have girlfriends?"

What was he saying? Had he wanted me all this time? The same way I'd wanted him.

"Really?"

He nodded his head. "Tell me, do you want me? Because the minute I wrap my arms around you to help you up, I won't let go unless you tell me no now."

"Jake..."

I wanted to tell him yes, but I didn't want to disappoint him in bed. If he was another man unable to give me orgasms, would it ruin everything between us? Was our friendship and roomie status worth risking on a night of unsatisfactory sex?

"Yes?"

"I don't know." The words stuck in my throat. Could the night get any more embarrassing?

"What don't you know? Do you like me?"

"You know I like you. Can't we have this conversation while dressed and sitting up?" Instead of his warm, enticing breath brushing over my stomach?

"Do you like me, like me?" He raised an eyebrow. "Or do I need to remind you that you were checking out my package earlier?"

"It's hard to miss." I tried to shrug, but my stuck arm prevented me.

"Answer the question."

"Yes, all right, yes," I huffed. "But..."

"But? What? Help me out here."

"But I don't want to disappoint you," I admitted in a quiet voice.

"How would you?"

"Well... I... ah... oh, hell, this is so embarrassing. I can't orgasm with a man."

His eyebrows rose, then lowered as heat filled his eyes once again.

"You haven't been with the right man then."

I chewed my bottom lip. Should I risk everything to find out if he was the right man? Risk our friendship? Our roommate? Because I was sure he'd move out if it didn't work out between us.

"Yes or no? Because I'm so fucking hard right now. Either I help you up and see if I can give you an orgasm or I help you up and I go give myself one."

Holy hell, that was hot thinking of him stroking himself and bringing himself to release, but as hot as that was, I wanted to be the one to make him come.

"Yes."

"Thank fuck for that," he muttered and slid his arms under my back.

A fire scorched a trail along my back and then my front as he dragged me to him and lifted me onto the bed. My leather-clad chest pressed against his Lycra-clad one. Every firm groove pressed into me, and my nipples hardened. I landed on the bed on top of him, my naked bottom half pushed down on him, the tights leaving no doubt how hard he was. He slid a hand to my naked butt and ground against me, hard. Sparks shot out of my clit, and I dry-humped him in need.

"Em, stop." He groaned. "You'll make me come."

A desperate need filled me. If I made him come, perhaps I wouldn't disappoint him when I didn't come. I moved faster and harder. He flipped us over in a swift move. My back hit the mattress and his mouth landed on mine in a drugging, desperate kiss of passion. Firm, demanding lips and hard thrusts of his tongue made me pull him closer. I wanted to climb inside his skin, make him feel the burning fire he'd flared to life inside me.

He pulled back with a groan and wrenched the zip down on the front of my Batman top. My breasts spilled free of the tight confines of the leather. He dipped his head to draw my aching nipple into the heat of his mouth.

"Jake," I cried as he switched to the other aching tip.

"You smell like leather," he said, raising his head. "Let's get this off, hey?"

"Please."

The top was almost as difficult as the pants, but he pulled the sleeves free, leaving me bare to him. Underwear beneath the damn costume had been impossible. Still dressed in his Robin costume, I reached for the hem of his top and moved it up to his chest. I stopped halfway, marveling at the sculpted firmness of his six-pack. I leaned forward and ran my tongue along the ridge, making his muscles tighten further.

"Damn, Em, I've never wanted anyone as much as I want you."

"Take your Robin costume off."

"After I give you your first orgasm."

"First?"

"Yep, first of many for the night."

"Jake..." I warned. I didn't want to disappoint him.

He pressed me back into the mattress with another drugging kiss. My heart rate soared, and blood pounded in my ears. He trailed his lips to my neck and swiped his tongue along my rapidly beating pulse. Even that sent a flood of moisture seeping from me. His lips sampled every sensitive place on my body, my shoulder, the curve of my breast, and teased around my nipples until they were begging for his mouth, but he continued down my body to my stomach clenched with my ragged breathing. His lips hit my hip, and I shook with need. He traced the length of my hip bone with his tongue, and I coiled tighter. My core clenched in desperate need of release from the rising tension.

I slid my hand to his short hair. The bristles tickled my palm as I ran my hand over his head, encouraging him to keep going. Keep heading to where his words ignited the burning desire. He pressed his nose to my pussy and inhaled.

"Like a ripe peach."

His lips moved close to where I wanted them to touch. Where I needed him to touch. To relieve this ache and achieve the impossible. To bring me to orgasm. I was so close that if I reached down with my fingers, I'd come with two strokes, but I wanted to experience it with someone else. Not just someone, but Jake. My heart constricted with the thought.

He swiped his tongue along my opening and over my clit.

"Oh, Jake." I was so close that the anticipation was agonizing.

"You taste like peaches too," he said, lips pressed against me.

He pushed his tongue in deep and fucked me with it. In and out he thrust his tongue, the sensation was exquisite along my tight walls clamping down on him. Closer and closer I got, but it was—as always—just out of my reach. He stopped and looked at me with hooded eyes.

"Em, talk to me."

"I can't do it," I sobbed. "It doesn't matter what you do. I won't come."

He chuckled. "Sorry, I wasn't trying to make you come. I was enjoying you too much."

"You weren't?"

"Nope, this time I will."

He pressed a finger into me deep and found a spot that brought white-hot pleasure to my body. My legs quivered with each massage of his finger, and I once again coiled tight to the point of release.

So close, so freaking close.

"Stop overthinking it." His warm breath brushed over me. "Relax and enjoy. If you get there great, if you don't, it means I need to learn more about how to please you."

No man had ever told me it was his fault if I didn't achieve an orgasm. My heart swelled with the suppressed feelings I had for Jake.

His tongue lapped at my clit. One lick, two. Relaxing into his hold, I closed my eyes and let the sensation of his tongue wind me tighter to the pinnacle of pleasure. Letting the sensations overwhelm me, and all thoughts of my past failures vanished.

"Yes," I cried.

Another lick of his tongue on oversensitive flesh and a curl of his finger and I came with a force that bowed my back off the bed. My legs jerked in time to the waves of pleasure bursting from my core.

"Holy hell, Jake, you did it." I pulled on his short hair.

He lifted his head and grinned at me.

"I said I would. Didn't I?"

"You did." What did this mean? Was Jake the right man? For me?

"Now for orgasm two." He smirked and returned his mouth to my clit and sucked.

"Jake!"

His mouth worked me up to another orgasm faster than I thought possible after coming so hard already. He spread my legs. His hands were firm, as though my body was now his to learn and enjoy. Baring me wide to his ministrations on my clit and opening,

I lay back, relaxed, and enjoyed him. In two minutes flat, I was coming against his mouth again.

I flopped back on the bed, my muscles a pile of satisfied goo, my lungs labored and breath coming in sharp rasps of exertion. He stood from the bed, and I opened my eyes. Damn, he was sexy with his confident smirk in place. He deserved to look so self-confident since he was the only man to ever give me an orgasm. Make that two and by the look in his eyes, he was aiming for a third.

Desire sparked back to life again the moment he lifted Robin's top over his head. Oh, wow. He slid the tights from his legs, and that thought turned to holy hell as he released his enormous erection in all its amazing hard glory. I might get lockjaw if I tried to suck him, but I wanted to find out. I scooted to the side of the bed and wrapped my hand around him, and lowered my mouth over the head of his erection. Salty pre-cum touched my tongue, and I lapped it while hollowing my mouth and bringing some of his length deep into my mouth to hit the back of my throat.

A sexy, deep groan rumbled from Jake's chest. He threaded his fingers into my bun and tugged my head away.

"Condoms?"

"Bedside drawer," I said, eager to feel his hard length inside me, and not just my mouth.

He reached for the drawer and fetched a foil packet, ripped it open, and rolled it on himself. Damn, it looked like a tight fit. I'd need to buy extra-large next time. Would there be a next time?

"Top or bottom?"

"It doesn't matter. I won't come either way."

"You're doubting me after two orgasms?"

"Do you think you're a Sex God?" I tried to shrug off my past failures, but I didn't want to get my hopes up. I didn't want to disappoint him, either.

He smirked. "Just call me Orgasm God."

He pulled me to him and kissed me senseless again, pushing away all my doubts and making need curl hard and deep in my stomach. His subtle chest hair brushed against my nipples and breasts, making them full and needy.

He broke the kiss. "Turn around."

At that moment, I would have jumped through a hoop for him. I turned around on the bed and he ran a hand up my back and cupped the back of my neck. He pushed gently until my face met the mattress and my ass was in the air.

"Fuck, your pussy is pretty special. Look at it, begging me to fill it."

"Yes, Jake, yes," I panted into the mattress.

He pushed my legs apart and nudged his flared head into my slick core. I was so wet with the need for him and my two previous orgasms that he slid in as though he weren't huge. A shudder ran along my spine, and he pulled back and pressed in again so slowly I felt every millimeter along my aching core. Slow and torturous, he fucked me, building the pressure so slowly and completely that my mind thought of nothing except the next slide of his hard cock deep inside me.

It could have been hours or minutes. I didn't know, so lost in pleasure and the building orgasm. His fingers found my clit and strummed it in time to his thrusts. My legs shook and a blinding roaring pleasure filled every inch of my body, from the inside to the outside and everything in between. There was nothing but Jake and the pleasure.

His cock swelled and hit that sweet spot of tight muscles that made my head spin with pleasure. I came with him buried deep.

"Jake! I love you," I yelled as the words ripped from my lungs with the force of my orgasm.

He slammed his hips into the soft curves of my ass, buried himself deeper, and exploded along with my orgasm. Jet after jet of pulsing release hit my spasming muscles. I almost blacked out from the pleasure of finally experiencing an orgasm during sex.

He pulled out, and I collapsed on the bed. Shit, did I tell him I loved him? Did he think it was the orgasm talking? I heard him disappear into the bathroom and then he joined me on the bed, wrapped his arms around me, and spooned me from behind. Damn, he was still semi-hard. Did that mean he'd go again? I didn't think I could.

His fingers tugged on my nipple and a delicious ripple pooled to my core. Guess I'd give it another go. I was with the right man, after all. A man I'd lusted after for way too long.

We fell into an exhausted sleep at some stage in the morning.

My bedroom door flew open and Nat barged in.

"Emily! Help! Do you have any condoms? I've run out."

I sat up with a start, pulling the sheet with me and revealing Jake.

She halted. "About time you two admitted your feelings for each other."

"I... we... ah, don't." Oh, hell, damn, Nat. "What do you mean?"

She pressed her hands to her hips. "Right, so, Conrad and I will just hop in bed with you guys..."

"Hell no!" Jake and I said together.

"Exactly, you idiots." She crossed to my open bedside drawer. "I'll just take a few of these," she said with a smirk and left the room. "Don't worry, Conrad and I don't share either. I was only pressing your buttons."

Jake brushed my long hair which was now free from its bun over my shoulder and pressed a kiss against my skin.

"Bloody Nat." He mocked a scowl. "I love you. Do you? Or do I need to remind you what you said earlier?"

"I... ah..."

"Yes or no?" He raised an eyebrow.

"Yes, all right, yes." There was no point denying I'd meant it.

"Thank fuck for that," he muttered and trailed his lips over my chest. "Now, what number of orgasms were you up to?"

"I lost count," I breathed out. It didn't matter how many orgasms he'd given me as I was certain he would give me many more in our future together. "Four?"

"I can do better than that." He huffed as though I'd offended him.

"Jake, four is a miracle." I threaded my fingers into his hair and tugged until his eyes met mine. "Thank you."

"You don't need to thank me."

"But you rescued me from thinking it was my fault."

"Em, it was never your fault." He kissed my neck.

"You've proven it wasn't, so thank you." I leaned over and kissed his forehead.

His mouth opened but both our phones buzzed loudly in the room with messages. Our gazes locked and then we scrambled from the bed to fetch them from the floor. My hand shook as I opened the text message. A grin slowly formed.

"I got the part!"

"Congratulations," Jake said sounding sad.

"Wait, didn't you get it?" I lowered my phone after reading the message again.

He pouted.

"Oh no, I'm sorry, Jake."

"Kidding." He grinned. "I got the part too."

"Jerk." I narrowed my eyes.

Jake laughed. "You didn't expect things to change too much, did you?" he asked, stalking toward me.

I backed up, hitting the mattress with the back of my knees, and fell onto the bed.

"I'll get you back."

"Can't wait." He lowered himself over my naked body. "No hair remover cream though. We both need to look the best for the television show."

"Right," I said, sliding my hands to his shoulders. "How about I make breakfast?"

Jake laughed. "And have you put a laxative in it? No way. I'm taking you out for a breakfast date."

"A date?"

"Yep. That's what boyfriends do. Take their girlfriends on dates."

"Oh, Jake." I hugged him to me hard.

"Right after I give you orgasm number four," he whispered into my ear.

"Fine by me." I grinned, the happiest I'd ever been with a man. A man I'd been friends with, a man I'd lived with, a man I'd had my first orgasm with. Jake was right, I'd needed the right man, and he was it.

"Lustman coming to the rescue again."

"Lustman?" I asked, biting my lip to stop laughing.

"It's my superhero name now." He grinned.

"Right. I'll have to get you a costume."

"No more costumes." He groaned. "Besides, I'm in it now and about to be in yours, Lustwoman."

I cracked up laughing. Roommate to boyfriend and I couldn't be happier and neither was Jake going by the way he laughed with me.

Read Claire and Travis's story in The Lust Giving the sixth book in the Hollywood Hearts series.

Afterword

Thank you so much for reading Lustman to
the Rescue.
Did you love my story?
Review it!

A reader who writes a review for a book
is a tremendous gift to the author. It lets
me know that someone read my book and
enjoyed the story enough to tell me. If you
enjoyed this book, please leave a review. I'd
be forever grateful.

Acknowledgments

First, thank you to my family for putting up with me disappearing into the world of books. To Belinda, thank you for encouraging me to write again after I lost everything in a computer crash. Remember to back up! A lot of work goes into creating a story, and I'm always thankful for the support of my online writing buddies, beta readers, and fellow authors, Immy for always making me smile, Tammy for believing in me from the start, Karen for being willing to read any level of heat I write. Cassie for her hand holding. Lana for her invaluable knowledge. Also, my fabulous beta reader Erica and her help with US English. The biggest thank you goes to my 'twin' Dannielle, who is

LUSTMAN TO THE RESCUE

the best critique partner, cheerleader, and sounding board ever, and is forever fixing my comma errors, sorry Dannielle I'm afraid you're stuck with them and me. Finally thank you to all you romance readers. You are my tribe.

About Author

Helen Walton is a tea drinking, chocoholic, romance writer. Stories are her obsession. She adores creating sensual romances containing a sprinkling of humor and the all-important happy ending. She lives in South Australia with her family, and menagerie of quirky animals where they all take her away from her book world and demand to be fed. Lucky for them, she enjoys cooking but prefers baking.

Sign up for my newsletter for exclusive content.

https://www.helenwaltonauthor.com/newsletter
Visit my website

https://www.helenwaltonauthor.com/

Follow me

BB bookbub.com/profile/helen-walton

f facebook.com/Helen-Walton-Author-1 03496667706602/

g goodreads.com/author/show/20249188 .Helen_Walton

◉ instagram.com/helen.walton.author

♪ tiktok.com/@helen.walton.author

HELEN WALTON

Also By

HELEN WALTON

LUSTMAN TO THE RESCUE

Anthologies

Reluctant Bride

Alpha Male